Oscar's Gift

Planting Words with
Oscar Micheaux

Lisa Rivero

Fiction for Young Historians

To young oddballs everywhere

Summary: At the beginning of the 20th century on the Rosebud Indian Reservation in South Dakota, eleven-year-old Tomas, a son of Swedish immigrants, befriends future novelist and film maker Oscar Micheaux as they both begin new lives as homesteaders.

Cover photo: A boy ploughing at Dr. Barnardo's Industrial Farm, Russell, Manitoba, ca. 1900.
Back photo: Oscar Micheaux (1884-1951), American film director, novelist, and homesteader

ISBN-10: 1466215593

ISBN-13: 978-1466215597

Contents

Acknowledgements

This book was made possible by a special birthday gift of words from my son, who encouraged me to start small and to follow my bliss. I am grateful to him and to my husband for their continual love and support, as well as to *Oscar's Gift*'s first readers and cheerleaders, especially Zeki, Katie, Brianne, Mark, Rachel, Charlie, and Jane. A particular note of appreciation goes to Jerry Wilske, Director of the Oscar Micheaux Center in Gregory, South Dakota, for reviewing the manuscript for historical accuracy and providing valuable background information. Some of the many published works that informed this story include Oscar Micheaux's novels *The Conquest: The Story of a Negro Pioneer* and *The Homesteader*; *The Great and Only*, by Patrick McGilligan; and *Writing Himself into History*, by Pearl Bowser and Louise Spence.

Part I

160 Acres

TROOPS ORDERED TO
START FOR BONESTEEL

Vigilantes Round Up 100 Bad Men
and Ship Them Away

DUMPED ON NEBRASKA PRAIRIE

South Dakota Town Patrolled by
200 Determined Citizens

Land-Seekers Will Be Protected

~ *New York Times* Headline, July 24, 1904

Chapter One

Land Lottery

I first saw Oscar on a hot July day in 1904, two months before my twelfth birthday. Mama and I had just arrived on a stage coach in Bonesteel, South Dakota. We were walking past the train station when a man a full head taller than everyone else stepped out of a passenger car. His skin was darker than I got by the end of the summer. Darker than Joe Squirrel Coat who sometimes did work at our boarding house. As dark as a moonless night.

"Don't stare, Tomas. It is not polite," Mama said. She grabbed my shirt sleeve and pulled me closer to her. Being polite was something my mama was most keen on. She never missed a chance to point out what was polite and what wasn't.

I tried not to stare, but how could I not? He carried himself even taller than he was. He looked down from the shade of his wide-brimmed hat at the people around him who stared back. He seemed used to being stared at.

He carried a brown leather satchel. His clothes were unlike any clothes I'd seen before. The high starched collar of his shirt was whiter than chalk. He wore a dark jacket with tiny stripes and matching vest, and a tie. I looked down at my own gray shirt, frayed at the cuffs and elbows, and my dirty dungarees.

When I looked up, he was gone.

The crowd brushed up against us as thick as grasshoppers. Folks had been coming to Bonesteel for days to participate in the land lottery, and all of the waiting had made people jumpy. That's why Mama and I were there, to get a lottery number in hopes of getting one of the over two thousand free land claims. It's what Papa had wanted.

This land on the Rosebud Indian Reservation in Gregory County was Indian land, but now white folks like us could have our own claim, that is if we were lucky in the lottery and we promised to live on the land for five years.

Across the street, some men were brawling and yelling. Two men wrestled on the ground, calling each other "cheater" and "swindler." Other men were standing in a circle around them, watching and cheering. Some of the men were holding rifles. Mama held the papers she carried closer to her stomach. I wanted to hold Mama's hand, but I was past the age of doing that.

Not every man who came to Bonesteel that summer was a good man. Mama read in the newspaper about pickpockets and thieves and gamblers—she called them the bad element. They came to the town to take advantage of all the rich people who were coming for land.

The problem was that most of the folks coming for the lottery were not rich. They were like us, families who had nothing but hope for a homestead and a need for a fresh start. This made the bad element angry. Some of them had been in Bonesteel for a year, expecting to get rich in ways that weren't lawful. When that didn't happen, they started fights and looted stores and fired rifles at houses.

Mama saw me staring across the street and poked my arm. I turned away. I didn't like crowds or lots of noise. To keep my mind occupied, I concentrated on listening to the voices around me. The voices were like a strange song of different languages and melodies.

I recognized that some of the people were speaking Swedish, the language that Mama used to speak to Papa late at night when they thought I was asleep. I also could pick out German and Russian, because guests at the boarding houses where we stayed sometimes spoke those languages. I recognized all these tongues and could tell them apart, but I only understood the voices in English.

"The governor is gonna send in the state troops soon if things don't settle down."

"Did the police chief really quit?"

"That's what I heard."

"I heard there was a gun fight a mile east of town."

"A bunch of town folks decided to take the law into their own hands, to be vigilantes."

"I heard that the vigilantes gathered up a hundred of them hooligans in a cattle car yesterday. Shipped them south, to Nebraska. Dumped 'em on the prairie."

"Good riddance is what I say. This here's a good town, a quiet town. We don't need no scalawags or trouble."

"Well, we got trouble whether we want it or not."

Mama stopped walking. I looked up.

The dark man stood in front of us. His figure blocked the afternoon sun. He touched the fingers of his free hand to the brim of his hat and bowed his head.

"Ma'am," he said. Then he looked at me and nodded. "Sir."

No one had ever called me sir before. He looked back at Mama. "Would you be so kind as to tell me where the land office is?" he asked.

His voice was deep and rich and slow like low thunder before a storm that forces you to stop what you are doing and listen. Mama hesitated a moment, then said, "Why, yes, we are going there as well. You may walk with us, if you'd like."

He touched his hat again and smiled a broad smile. "Much obliged, Ma'am. My name is Oscar

Micheaux." He said his last name mee-show. "I've come on the train from Chicago to be a homesteader."

Mama didn't smile. She said simply, "Pleased to meet you, Mr. Micheaux," and continued walking. She didn't tell him our names. I wondered if this was the polite thing to do.

The human grasshoppers chirped and bumped against each other as we all made our way to the far side of town. Every so often I turned around to see Mr. Micheaux walking behind us, tall as a young spruce tree. He looked straight in front of him, over our heads. His being with us somehow made me feel safer from the bad element.

We walked for what seemed like all afternoon. I had never seen so many people in one place. Finally we reached a gray building with the words LAND OFFICE in white letters above the door. The line we were in led to a table and chairs set up in front of the door. Two men were seated at the table.

When Mama reached the table, she gave one of the men her papers. The man wore a tie like Oscar, but he had taken off his jacket and rolled up his shirt sleeves. His forehead was sweaty and his cheeks were red.

"Do you swear that you are at least twenty-one years of age?" he asked her, without looking up from his papers.

"Yes," she said.

"Do you now already own one hundred and sixty or more acres of land in any state or territory, or have you ever owned such land?" the man asked.

"No," she said.

"Sign here," he said. He handed her a pen. She signed her name. He gave her a card. When she didn't do anything, he tapped his finger on the card and said in an annoyed tone, "Write your address on this card."

Mama gave the pen to me to write the address of our boarding house.

Mama's family had come from Sweden to the United States on a ship when she was just a girl. Since living in the United States, Mama had learned to speak English, but not to write or read it, except for writing her name. I had helped her to learn to write her name as well as any American.

She didn't like people to know that she couldn't read or write. Papa used to do her reading and writing for her.

The man took the card from me. He wrote something on a piece of paper and gave the paper to Mama. She stepped to the side and folded the paper carefully. I knew she would ask me to read it to her once we were alone.

I looked for Mr. Micheaux to take his turn at the table. He was no longer behind us. I stood on my toes to try to see through the line of people. The crowd pushed us to the side.

Mama and I made our way back to the train station, where we would hire a stage coach to take us home. All the way I looked for Mr. Micheaux, but he had disappeared.

I didn't see him again for almost a year. Later he would tell me he went to a different town to put his name in for the lottery, a town that was less "crowded and lawless," as he put it, and that had nicer hotels. He would tell me to call him Oscar when my mama wasn't around (she said it wasn't polite to call adults by their first names). I learned that he was only twenty years old that summer, not twenty-one as he would have had to swear to for the lottery.

Before I met Oscar, I thought that life was a game of chance. Now you see it. Now you don't. Like the game with walnut shells Papa and I saw once at a county fair. A man put a tiny round stone under one of three walnut shells. Then he moved the shells left and right, over and under, back and forth so fast that I lost track of which shell had the stone. After he had finished moving the shells, people paid him money to guess which shell had the stone. If they guessed right, they got a prize. If they guessed wrong, they lost their money.

Papa didn't bet on the shell game. He wasn't a gambling man, but he and I would watch others place bets, and we made our own guesses between ourselves. No matter how closely I watched and how sure I was that I had kept my eye on the right shell, I always guessed wrong. Papa did, too.

I used to think that life was like that walnut shell game. It didn't matter how hard I tried or how much I hoped. In the end, whether I chose the right shell was pure luck. Sometimes things worked out. Sometimes they didn't. Mostly they didn't.

Chapter Two

Birthday Surprise

The postcard arrived in September on my birthday. The summer had passed quickly after the day of the land lottery, and school had begun only weeks before.

That day Miss Farnsworth asked me to stay after the other children went home. I had been to a lot of schools in different towns in the past several years, and Miss Farnsworth was my favorite teacher and the one I'd had the longest. Whenever I finished my work early or already knew what she was going to teach, she gave me extra books to read or asked me to help one of the other pupils. She never scolded or grew impatient, and she knew about parts of the world I had never been to or even known about before.

She was also very pretty, with golden hair drawn up in a bun. Her full skirts floated just above the ground as she walked. When she smiled at me, I worked harder, just to see her smile more. Papa had said I was lucky that no young man had married her yet, because once she was married, she would stop teaching to have her own family. I hoped Miss Farnsworth never got married.

Papa had been as keen on schooling as Mama was on manners. Whenever we came to a new town, the first thing he did was to find the school and meet the teacher. He said that he was working hard so that my life could be different from his. He wanted me to work with my head instead of my hands, and working with my head would take schooling.

Papa could read and write, but he didn't have much schooling. Like Mama, he had come from Sweden to the United States when he was young. He got a job with the railroad, laying tracks and driving spikes. For three years, Papa, Mama and I moved from town to town as he built the rails. Every few months we packed up our few belongings and followed the new railroad farther west.

When Papa brought home a pamphlet from the railroad advertising land in what used to be Dakota Territory, he told us he would quit working for the railroad so that we could have a homestead and stay in one place.

"Look at this!" he said with excitement to Mama. The flyer showed a drawing of a man leading a pair of horses that were pulling a plow. Behind the plow, wheat sprung from the earth, but instead of regular wheat, this wheat had heads of gold coins. "Best Land for Farming!" the words promised. "Rich Soil!"

"We will finally have a home of our own, Sonja," he told Mama. He always said the "y" sound of her name with a special softness: sone-yah, like the coo of a mourning dove. I remember him standing behind her, his strong, suntanned arms wrapped around her small waist. "I'll be able to keep what I build for us, not leave it behind for others to use," he promised. She looked at him in a way that made me turn away, as if I'd seen a treasure I was not supposed to find.

He had talked about his plans for our future as though our lottery number had already been picked, as though he had kept his eye on the right shell all along.

I believed him. I worked even harder in school to make him proud of me. At night when noise from the other guests in the boarding houses kept me awake, I entertained myself by imagining our new life on our new homestead. We would stay in one place, and I would stay in one school. I would help Papa on the farm in the morning and evenings.

I imagined our big farmhouse. It would be painted white and have two stories and big windows. Instead of all of us sleeping in one room, I would have my own room with a big, soft bed. Mama would have her own kitchen, and we wouldn't have to eat with other boarders. The mornings would be quiet, without the sounds of horses and wagons on the streets or boarders coming in late.

Many nights I fell asleep imagining the future that Papa was planning for us, and that future continued in the stories of my dreams, so that when I woke up, I almost believed it had already come true until wakefulness settled fully on me.

Then, one day last winter, a man from the railroad company came to our door. He held his hat in one hand and a telegram and a pocket watch in the other. Mama said the way he held his hat to his chest was how she knew what he was going to say, even before he said it and before she saw Papa's watch.

Papa and two other men had got caught under a load of steel rails that fell off a wagon. Railroad workers had to be strong to drive spikes and haul wood ties, but they weren't strong enough to get out from under a load of steel.

After Papa died, we moved to a different boarding house, one that wasn't as nice as the one all three of us had lived in. Mama began working in the flour mill, filling flour sacks and sewing them shut. She worked all day, every day except Sunday. At the beginning, her fingers were red and cut from learning to use the sewing machines. She began to cough from breathing in flour all day. She never complained, but she was tired all the time now. And she never laughed anymore the way Papa could make her laugh.

These thoughts were going through my mind that day on my birthday, as I waited for the other children to go home after school. I was one of the oldest pupils in the school, and my knees bumped against the desk unless I stretched out my legs. Because no one was sitting in front of me now, I stretched my legs out as far as I could.

When I was the only student left, Miss Farnsworth gave me one of her smiles.

"I have something for you, Tomas," she said.

She reached into her desk and brought out a newspaper. She handed it to me.

"Take a look at this and tell me what you think."

The newspaper was called *The Youth's Companion*. It was dated August 18, 1904. The front page had a drawing of a man on a horse and the title of a story, "When the Savings Bank Was Robbed." Other stories were called "The Hero of Kettle Falls" and "The Crumpled Rose-Leaf" and "The Fall of a Sparrow."

Page after page—twelve pages in all—were filled with stories, some made up and some true. There was a photograph of President Teddy Roosevelt with his bushy mustache and wire-rim glasses. There was news about Russia and the Trans-Siberian Railway. A section called "Nature and Science" told of a German expedition to the South Pole, and described something called a cyclograph, "an instrument by means of which a bicyclist may make an automatic chart of his course through an unknown country."

There were poems and jokes, and advertisements for Edison Phonograph Records and Gold Medal Flour and a Liquid Pistol, guaranteed to "stop the most vicious dog (or man) without permanent injury."

I had never seen anything so fine and told her so. "You can keep this newspaper for free," she said. "And if you give me five cents every week, I can give you a new one."

She said I could read each issue and study it at home, and in school she would help me learn to write like the writers whose words were on the pages. She also said that if Mama didn't have five cents a week to spare, I could work a little after school each day to earn the money, erasing chalk boards and cleaning the school building.

I wondered if Mama had told her it was my birthday, and that was why she was giving me this newspaper, but then she said, "Tomas, I'm giving this to you because you have a gift with words. It would be a shame for you not to learn how to use your gift. I want to show what you wrote about Bonesteel to the editor of the newspaper. He is my uncle, and he might have a need for an apprentice."

The week before she had asked all of the pupils to write a story about something we had seen or done over the summer. I wrote about "The Battle of Bonesteel" from the day of the land lottery two months before. I always remember everything I see and hear. Papa used to say it was uncanny how I remembered things. My story began, "As one man in the street said, 'We got trouble whether we like it or not.'"

"What I liked about your story was how you described the heroism of the townsfolk as well as the acts of the outlaws," she was saying. "It takes a special eye to be able to see all sides of this world and to show both the bad and the good without unfairly choosing sides. It takes a writer's eye."

Miss Farnsworth said that I might be able to start apprenticing as early as next summer, but that I had a lot to learn before I could do a man's trade. Being an apprentice meant I would work without getting paid in money. My payment would be learning how to work with words. Then, when I had learned enough, I could get a job at a newspaper, maybe even the newspaper where I apprenticed.

"A boy like you has a different kind of future from a lot of others," she said. My cheeks burned, but I forced myself to keep looking at her. "You are lucky. But having a gift is not always easy. Other people don't always understand. They might be jealous or think you are wasting your time. You have to know what you want and be willing to work to get it, no matter what."

No one had ever talked to me this way before. It was true that sometimes I felt different from other children, but I didn't think it was because of any gift I had. I didn't like the games they played. When I tried to talk to them, they weren't interested in what I had to say, so eventually I stopped talking much at all. Mama said that because I didn't have brothers or sisters alive, I didn't know how to talk to children. I could talk just fine to older people, but grown folks usually didn't want to talk to me.

That's how I got to be such a good listener, by not talking and using my ears and eyes instead. It suited me just fine.

Me, a newspaper man.

I thanked her and told her I would ask Mama about the five cents every week. While I wasn't sure that we had that much extra money, I was willing to work after school, like Miss Farnsworth said.

I couldn't wait to tell Mama what the teacher had said. All the way home I thought about how I would write about everything that was happening around me. I would learn about our town and our state, which was only fifteen years old. I would get the facts by talking to folks, then put those facts in words everyone could understand. I would make enough money to buy Mama a house of her own in town. She could stop working at the flour mill. She would stop being so tired all the time. She might even laugh again.

When I turned the corner toward the boarding house, I saw Mama coming to meet me. She was walking fast, and she held a postcard. She was still wearing her work apron, and her hair was dusted white with flour.

My stomach tightened. Ever since the day the telegram was delivered, telling us about Papa, I knew that news could be bad. Worse than anything bad one could imagine.

"Tomas, we have a farm!"

Our number had been drawn in the lottery.

We walked together back to the boarding house. Mama was usually a very quiet woman, quieter than an Indian, Papa used to say, but this time she talked all the way. As she talked, I realized that I was looking down at her.

When did I get to be taller than Mama? I wondered at what point I would be taller than Papa had been.

"We need to hire us a locator," she was saying, "someone who can help us to find the best claim. We should look for a place with a hill for our house. That's what Joe—" She stopped for a moment, her face odd looking.

"That's what Mr. Squirrel Coat says. He read me the postcard," she explained. "He also offered to help build our house. And of course you will now do the work your father would have done." She put her hand on my shoulder. "You are a man now, Tomas. A farmer."

Me, a farmer.

Mama didn't ask me about the newspaper in my hand. That was the last day I went to school.

Chapter Three

A Great Sea of Grass

The very next day, Joe Squirrel Coat took Mama and me in his wagon to look at claims. Each homestead claim was called a quarter-section because it was one-fourth of a square mile, or one hundred and sixty acres.

Mr. Squirrel Coat was our locator. A locator was someone who knew the land and showed new homesteaders which claims were available. Homesteaders usually paid locators to help them find the best claim, but Mr. Squirrel Coat said he would be our locator for free.

Mr. Squirrel Coat worked for Mrs. Sully who owned the boarding house. There he fixed up broken windows, leaky walls, and loose floor boards. I never saw him get angry, not even when Mrs. Sully wanted him to work late into the night or very early in the morning, or when other boarders ordered him to help them carry bags as if he was a servant.

He was tall, but not as tall as Mr. Micheaux. His long black braids hung down his back like a girl, but that was the only thing like a girl about him. He was the only other man I knew who was as strong as Papa.

The wind blew so hard I had to hang onto the side of the wagon to keep from tipping over. All of the claims looked the same to me, a canvas of browns and greens dotted with purple and yellow. Except for us and our wagon and horses, the world looked as though it had just been born and we were the first people to see it.

As we rode along the prairie, Mr. Squirrel Coat pointed out the different plants and told us how to tell them apart. He explained that we should choose land that had fresh water, a hilly area for our house, and trees to shelter us from the wind. I didn't see many trees anywhere. We also should avoid land that had a lot of buffalo wallows, which were areas worn away by herds of buffalo that rolled on the ground. These low spots on the prairie would be hard to plow and would quickly fill with rain water, flooding any young crops.

The first claim he showed us was too flat for a dug-out house. We couldn't afford to build a house of wood, because wood needed to be shipped on a train, which was expensive. A house dug out from a hill would be cheaper to build and would give us good protection against the winter winds. Mr. Squirrel Coat said most homesteaders built dug-out houses or sod houses or a combination of both. He drove right past that claim without stopping.

The second claim wasn't as flat as the first claim, but it had a lot of buffalo wallows and didn't have any source of water on it. We wouldn't have a well on our claim, so we would need a source of fresh water to use for drinking and cooking and washing. Mr. Squirrel Coat said that lack of fresh water was the undoing of many homesteaders. We drove past that claim, too.

The third claim had both low hills on one end and a creek on the other. A few trees and wild fruit bushes grew next to the creek. Mr. Squirrel Coat said it was the best available claim for miles. It almost seemed as though he had this claim in mind all along. He said his own land was right next to it.

He didn't have to register for the lottery to get his claim. The Indians got their land because this land had all been theirs before white people ever came. I knew that Mr. Squirrel Coat was a farmer, and Mama had said that he knew a lot about getting land ready for planting, but I didn't know he had his own claim. I wondered how he learned to be a farmer. And I wondered who decided which of the claims no longer belonged to the Indians and now could belong to us.

We stopped on the edge of the third claim, near the hilly area. Mr. Squirrel Coat helped Mama off the wagon seat and walked with her to the low hill where our house would be. Mama turned to him and smiled as he talked. They seemed to forget that I was there.

I climbed out of the back of the wagon and started walking, too, but away from them. I knew I could walk the side of an acre in one hundred paces, because Miss Farnsworth had us do so last spring, and I knew that a quarter section was about twelve acres by twelve acres. Our claim would be about one thousand, two hundred paces across, or six hundred paces to the middle.

I counted my steps, careful to avoid tripping on prairie dog holes.

One. Two. Three. I picked up an old buffalo bone bleached white by the sun. I imagined how the buffalo had once feasted on this grass. Even before the Indians lived here, this was the buffalo's home. I threw the bone as far as I could, watching it spin through the air.

Sixty-eight. Sixty-nine. As I walked, I learned to lift my feet high to make my way through the matted grass. If I wasn't careful, the high wheat-grass twisted around my ankles and shoes.

Two hundred and five. Two hundred and six. A snake slithered ahead of me, vanishing almost as fast as it appeared. Mr. Squirrel Coat had told us that most snakes on the prairie, such as garter snakes and water snakes, were harmless, but that we would need to watch for deadly rattlesnakes, especially young ones, whose venom could kill even a grown man.

Three hundred and twenty. Three hundred and twenty-one. I saw an arrowhead half buried in the ground. I picked it up and put it in my pocket. The arrowhead was made of dark red stone and was very sharp at the point. I pretended I was a young Indian boy who had carved the arrowhead to use to hunt the buffalo that ate the buffalo grass. In my imagination, I would bring the slain buffalo back to my camp, where I would be cheered and where the buffalo would be used for meat and the hides for blankets and clothing.

Four hundred and fifty. Four hundred and fifty-one. Mosquitoes buzzed around my ears and bit me on my hands and face. Grasshoppers scattered at my feet with my every step. Prairie dogs poked their heads through the grass before popping back into their holes. Mr. Squirrel Coat had explained that prairie dogs weren't really dogs. There were rodents, like rats or gophers, but they barked like dogs. Prairie dogs were the favorite diet of many other animals, which is why the prairie dogs didn't stray far from their holes.

Five hundred and ninety-eight. Five hundred and ninety-nine. Six hundred. I stopped.

This was the middle of our claim.

I stood in the center of a great sea of grass. Everywhere I looked I saw the buffalo grass and milkweed plants that Mr. Squirrel Coat had pointed out along our journey. Wheatgrass moved in waves with the breeze. I recognized yellow wild sunflowers and black-eyed Susan, the white flowers of wild garlic and the purple flowers of phlox.

Everything I saw was ours. The only fence was the horizon, where the deep blue of the sky met the brown and green earth like a giant perfect circle drawn around me. I spread my arms and turned slowly around, lifting my face to the sun, allowing the wind to blow through me.

I thought, this was what Papa saw under the walnut shell.

Part II

Breaking Sod

"I am a red man.

If the Great Spirit had desired me

to be a white man

he would have made me so in the first place.

He put in your heart certain wishes and plans,

in my heart he put other and different desires.

Each man is good in his sight.

It is not necessary for Eagles to be Crows."

~ Sitting Bull

Chapter Four

Building Our Soddy

"Buffalo grass is good for two things: buffalo and houses," Mr. Squirrel Coat said. Buffalo grass grew everywhere on our claim. It was low and thick and curly. Its roots reached deep into the soil for moisture and did not let go.

Every morning Mr. Squirrel Coat picked me up at the boarding house in his wagon and took me to our claim. He and I had already dug into the side of a hill to make the inside of our house. The part of the hill that we hadn't dug would act as the north side of the house to give us shelter from the wind. The top of the hill would be part of our roof. The outer walls and rest of the roof would be made of buffalo grass. We would have a house made from our very own land.

"The top layer of grass is called sod," he said. "The grass weaves the land together like a blanket and it can be taken off like a blanket." He used his horses to pull a special plow to cut long strips of sod about four inches thick. I walked behind him, using a spade to cut the strips into pieces as wide as the span of my arms. We had been cutting sod for three days. Mr. Squirrel Coat plowed off strips of long green and brown blankets, and I cut them into big bricks of sod. We had almost enough bricks for a house.

I positioned the spade at the right spot on the strip of sod and stepped down hard on the top of the blade. Sweat dripped in muddy lines down my face and back. The sun was at the top of the sky, without a cloud to be seen.

We both had been working since early morning, but Mr. Squirrel Coat did not look tired. He wore a leather shirt, but he did not sweat. His long black braids weren't damp. He spoke little to me, a sentence or two at a time, but what he said was always interesting and never just to talk for the sake of talking. He didn't smile on the outside. Once in a while, though, I began to recognize a smile under his face, if I looked closely enough.

He learned to build sod houses—he called them soddies—from settlers and soldiers at the fort near the Missouri River. He also practiced his English with the settlers and soldiers. He spoke English better than Mama did and almost as well as I did.

He said he first learned English when he was a boy at the Carlisle Indian School in Pennsylvania. It was a boarding school, which meant he slept and lived there, instead of with his parents. The people at the school cut his hair and made him wear scratchy cloth shirts with buttons. They also gave him the name of Joseph and wouldn't let him speak his Indian language of Lakota. He was a quick learner and a good student.

Now that he was a man with his own place, he grew his hair long and wore the buckskin clothes of his people. "Carlisle wasn't all bad, but it wasn't all good, either," he said. "They said they needed to kill the Indian in us to save the man." He pointed to his chest. "The Indian and man are one and the same. They could not kill me, and I didn't need to be saved."

He said because he now knew English, some members of his own family no longer trusted him. They thought he had betrayed his roots and his people by learning ways of the white pioneers.

"We can all learn from each other," he said. "I did not become a white man just because I can read and write."

We stopped the horses and removed their harnesses. It was time to eat. The horses shook their heads and whinnied, letting the prairie breeze dry their sweaty necks and manes.

We sat in the shade of the plow. I drank sweet water from a jug until my stomach hurt. Then we ate bread and butter sandwiches prepared that morning by Mama. Mr. Squirrel Coat shared rich slabs of fry bread that were crisp and brown on the outside and soft on the inside. I used my pocket knife to cut crisp slices of green apples. Food never tasted as good as it did after a morning of plowing and cutting sod. No matter how tired I was before we stopped to eat, I was always ready to start work again after we put the harnesses back on the horses.

The next day we began laying the walls of the house. We put the sod bricks with the grass side down in layers of two, side by side, for walls two feet thick. After a few rows, we laid the bricks the other way. Then we switched again, so that after a while the wall looked like a checkerboard. This crisscross pattern made the walls strong.

One day Mr. Squirrel Coat had some wooden planks in the wagon. He used these to make a door and two window frames. Another day he brought posts and planks he had cut and hewn from a cedar tree. These were our support beams and rafters. Finally we laid a layer of sod on the roof. "Not too thick," he said, "or it will be so heavy it will fall on top of you."

"Now let's get the inside of this soddy ready for your mama," he said.

We swept out all the extra dirt from the floor and packed it hard with our feet. Mr. Squirrel Coat used his wagon to bring a table and three chairs from his house. He also brought two beds and a black stove he called a monkey stove. The stove was low and broad and flat on top. He said it was called a monkey stove because monkey meant small, and monkey stoves were used where other stoves were too big.

We moved all of this into the one room of our house. I stood in the room and thought it was perfect for two people, but I wondered what Mr. Squirrel Coat would use in his house after giving all of this furniture to us.

The night we finished our soddy, Mama washed her hair with egg yolks and brushed it until it shone. She laid out a dress I'd never seen before—a dark blue dress with white sleeves and flowers embroidered in orange and red and yellow thread. The flowers flowed from her shoulders down to the bottom of the dress like a flower waterfall. She said the dress had been her mama's from the old country. She mended the hem and tightened a loose button. Before she went to bed, she gave an envelope to Mrs. Sully and shook her hand.

The next morning, Mr. Squirrel Coat came to our boarding house, but not for me. He helped Mama into his wagon. He was wearing eagle feathers in his braids, and his shirt sparkled with colorful porcupine quills.

When Mama and Mr. Squirrel Coat came back in the evening, two girls wrapped in woolen shawls were riding in the back of the wagon. They looked at me with large black eyes.

"Tomas, Mr. Squirrel Coat and I are man and wife," Mama said. "You can call him Papa now. These are your new sisters."

I didn't care if it was rude to stare. I stared at Mama until my eyes burned, until my head screamed, until the words I could not say would somehow find their way into her ears.

I would never call him Papa. And I knew my only brother and sister died before I was born, when they were just babies. Mama had told me so. I continued to stare as I climbed in the wagon next to these two strange girls, headed to what I had thought would be Mama's and my home, to the home that Papa had promised her and that I was going to give her.

Now you see it. Now you don't.

Chapter Five

The Long Winter

I never did call Mr. Squirrel Coat "Papa." I decided to call him Joe. I didn't care if it wasn't polite.

Joe and I built a sod barn in the same way we had built the house, except the barn was all sod and wasn't dug from a hill. The rest of the fall and into the early winter, we broke sod.

Buffalo grass may have been good for houses, but it was bad for farming. We needed to break it up and plow it under to expose the soil underneath before we could plant crops in the spring. Joe's horses pulled a breaker plow with a slanted blade to cut through the sod, but instead of lifting the sod up in strips as we did for the soddy, we turned it over and plowed through it again.

Every homesteader for miles and miles was breaking sod that fall, racing to break as many acres as they could before the ground froze. I worked from sunrise until it was too dark to see, stopping only to pick up old buffalo bones and rocks too big to be plowed under. We piled the bones and rocks next to our soddy. At night I lay down on a corn husk mattress next to the girls' bed and fell asleep before I could think a single thought.

During the coldest winter months I had time to get used to our new family. The girls' names were Winona and Chumani. They seemed invisible most of the time, except when they spoke to their father—they called him ah-tay—in Lakota. They could sit so quiet and still, doing beadwork or helping Mama sew, that I often forgot they were there.

Winona was nine years old. She was small and thin, like a prairie flower. Chumani was six years old, but she was tall and sturdy, and almost as big as her older sister. Someone who didn't know them would think they were the same age.

Mama told me that in the Lakota language the name Winona means first-born daughter, and

Chumani means dew drop. Winona was quiet and thoughtful, like her father. Chumani smiled more and sometimes laughed, then quickly covered her mouth with her hand.

Their mother had died when Chumani was born. "They have the same loss you have, Tomas. You should pity them," Mama said, whenever I refused to look at them or talk to them.

I wondered what it would be like not to have known Papa, not to have a memory of his blue eyes or his scratchy beard or the way he smelled when he smoked his pipe. Even though Papa wasn't with us, I could close my eyes and see him whenever I wanted.

I knew I should pity the girls, but I couldn't. They didn't know what it was like to have someone in your life one minute, and gone the next. It wasn't the same at all. They were not my sisters.

When the blizzard winds howled, we huddled under quilts and blankets toward the back of our soddy, away from the drafty door and windows. Mama burned sunflower stalks and corn cobs and even cow chips sometimes to keep us warm. We ate a lot of beans and potatoes and bread.

Joe set steel traps on our claim and checked them every day. Whenever he caught a beaver or a skunk or a raccoon, he skinned it and hung the fur inside the soddy. Soon our room was filled with furs of all sizes and colors. In the spring he would take them to town to sell.

The winter was long. We had no work we could do, no places to go, no books to read. Whenever there was enough moonlight at night, I moved my straw mattress next to the window, removed the paper over the window that kept out the wind, and read my copy of *The Youth's Companion*.

I learned news about a place called Panama where our country was building a canal. I read about an invention of a portable wireless telegraph that hunters could carry with them. I learned that Halsted Street in Chicago is thought to be the longest paved street in the world. I wondered if Mr. Oscar Micheaux had ever walked on Halsted Street and if he ever got his homestead claim.

I even read all of the advertisements. My mouth watered for Horlick's Malted Milk, "Pure, rich milk and the extract of selected malted grain." I studied the drawings of made-to-order women's suits, wishing I could give one to Mama. I pined for Hard Knocks Shoes for Boys: "Look Well – Wear Better," the ad promised. My own shoes were pinching at my toes and left me with hard calluses.

But the best part of the newspaper was the stories. There I lost myself in tales of travel and heroism and adventure. By the end of the winter, I had read every story several times, and the paper was beginning to tear where it was folded over.

Sometimes, while I was reading, I noticed Chumani looking at me from under her blanket. I knew she wished I would put the paper back on the window and go to sleep. I turned my back to her and continued to read.

When I emerged from the soddy in the spring, I was no longer the child who wished he could hold his mama's hand. Since moving onto our claim last fall, I'd grown taller. The work of breaking sod had changed me. I sometimes didn't recognize my own arms and legs, now hard and strong. My shoes felt even tighter than they had in the fall. They hurt so much that I had to go barefoot until Mama gave me a pair of Papa's old work boots. The boots were too

big, and after a day of work I pulled them off to re-
veal painful blisters that oozed and bled.

The first thing Joe did after the long winter
was to buy a milk cow. Mama named her Maggie.
She had brown skin, a pleasant face and a soft,
white belly.

Joe made me a milking stool by joining two
boards into a tee shape. I sat on the top of the tee,
using my feet and the bottom of the tee for balance.
It was my job every morning to milk Maggie, then
take her to the end of the claim where there was
good grass for grazing. At night I found her,
brought her back to the barn and milked her again.

At first I didn't know how to milk a cow. She
tried to kick me or butt me with her head whenever
I pulled at her udders. I learned to rest my head
and shoulder against her side as I milked, to let her
know where I was. Once we got used to each other,
she released her milk freely and I was able to milk
her quickly. Her milk tasted like sweet prairie grass
and was the best thing I had tasted in a long time.

I was coming back from taking Maggie to pas-
ture one morning when I saw a dark figure riding
toward our house on a white horse. He rode tall in

his saddle, his chin high and his arms loose. He wore a cowboy hat, a white shirt, new dungarees, and red kerchief around his neck. He rode to meet me and swung his long legs easily off the horse's back. He looked at me and smiled.

"Well, I'll be!" He looked me up and down. "Do you remember me?" he asked.

I nodded.

"Is your mama home?"

I nodded again and ran inside the house. "Mama! Mr. Micheaux is here!"

I could tell she didn't recall him at first. Then her eyes opened wide with remembering. "Stay inside," she said to Winona and Chumani. She wiped her hands on her apron and used her hand to smooth her hair before going outside.

"Mr. Micheaux," she said. "How nice to see you again."

He removed his hat and bowed. "Likewise, ma'am," he said.

He used his hat to point in the direction he had come from. "My homestead is just a couple of claims over from yours," he said. "I am riding around the country to meet my neighbors."

He told us about registering for the lottery in the town of Chamberlain instead of Bonesteel. When the lottery numbers were drawn, Mr. Micheaux's was six thousand, five hundred and four. That was too high for a chance at a claim. He didn't give up, though. He waited a few months and was able to buy a claim that someone else got but didn't want. He called it a relinquished claim, because the first person relinquished it or gave it up.

Mama asked him to come inside, to sit down and have something to eat.

"I would prefer to stay outside, Ma'am, if you don't mind. I'm right comfortable here."

He looked toward the soddy. "But I would be most happy to have some of what smells so delicious from your kitchen and some milk," he said.

Mama seemed surprised, but she nodded and went inside. She returned with half a loaf of our fresh morning bread and a jar. She gave the jar to me. I went to the barn and used a metal ladle to pour some of Maggie's fresh milk from the milk pail into the jar.

I gave this warm milk to Oscar, who had already finished the bread. He drank the milk all at once without stopping, then wiped his mouth on his sleeve and returned the jar to me.

"Thank you kindly, Ma'am. That was a most delicious dessert."

I had never known anyone before or since who called bread and milk a dessert. I wondered what he would think of the cookies Mama used to make, back when we had butter and sugar and walnuts. The more I thought of those cookies, the more my mouth wanted one. Oscar would never ask for bread and milk again if he could taste one of Mama's cookies.

Oscar talked for a while longer, asking about our claim, how we built our house and barn, and what crops we planned to sow.

"Ma'am," Oscar said before he left, "I don't recall having learned your names."

"My name is Sonja Squirrel Coat," Mama said. She pointed to me. "This is Tomas. My husband, Joe, is in town today. The girls are inside." Oscar looked toward the soddy, where Winona and Chumani were peeking through one of the windows.

Oscar frowned, just a little. I wasn't sure Mama even noticed, but I did. "Well, Mrs. Squirrel

Coat, I'd be happy if you and your son would come and visit me sometime. I am just over that ridge. You can follow the creek." He looked at me. "I could use another pair of strong hands to help me with my house. It looks like your boy Tomas here is a good worker, and I would pay handsomely."

"Thank you, Mr. Micheaux," Mama said. "I will ask my husband. We will see."

He then shook my hand, tipped his hat to Mama, and mounted his horse. I watched him ride back toward his place until he disappeared over a low hill.

That's how I came to work for Oscar Micheaux.

Chapter Six

Oscar

All that spring and summer I worked in the mornings and most of the afternoons with Joe. As soon as the ground thawed, we used a horse-pulled machine called a disc harrow to cut through the sod we had broken the previous fall. The disc harrow had round metal discs that rolled through the earth to make it soft and crumbly for planting.

We also continued to break new sod whenever we could. We had broken about forty acres so far. Joe wanted to break eighty acres by winter. We set aside part of our land for alfalfa, which Joe said would eventually be the feed for the hogs he planned to raise.

We built a chicken shed and a hog pen next to the barn. Joe bought a sow that Mama named

Emma. She was fat and lazy and would be the mother of hogs someday. Joe said that next spring he would buy baby chicks so that we could have fresh eggs to eat and to sell. We would butcher the grown chickens to eat.

In addition to all of this work with land and animals, there were always repairs to be made to the soddy. Sometimes snakes and other creatures would crawl through the walls and make holes. Other times rain would soak through the roof and drip on us while we were sleeping. The floor was always dusty, even though Mama swept it several times a day. She tried to use cloth for a rug, but it got so muddy that she preferred to sweep the hard dirt floor.

Winona and Chumani worked just as hard as I did. Twice a day they walked to the creek with pails to get fresh water. They peeled potatoes and baked bread and washed clothes. Mama said they were the best helpers in the world.

At about three o'clock every afternoon I walked to Oscar's place. There I worked until sunset, when I went home to milk Maggie.

Oscar and I built his soddy and a barn and what he called his necessary house—what I called his outhouse or toilet. At the end of every week, he gave me two dollars. I gave the money to Mama.

Oscar had enough money to build a wooden frame for his soddy and barn, which made them stronger than most sod buildings. He had also already bought his own horse and a wagon for travel.

He told me he got the money by working as a Pullman Porter with the railroad. He had saved two thousand dollars so that he could buy a relinquished claim.

"I always have a plan if things don't work out the first time," he told me. "When I didn't get lucky in the lottery, I just worked more and saved more money. It turned out I had more than enough money. A girl from east of the Missouri River owned this land first, so I went to visit her and her family. I dickered them down to three hundred and seventy-five dollars." He was proud of his dickering skills.

Oscar was the first and best storyteller I've ever known. While we worked, he told me all kinds of stories about his life. Later, I sometimes wondered how many of them were true, since he had no trouble lying about his age to get his claim, but at the time I chose to believe every word.

My favorite stories were about the railroad. Whenever Oscar talked about being a Pullman Porter, I imagined him travelling on some of the very tracks Papa had laid.

Papa had told me about Pullman Company Sleeper Cars. Pullman cars were train cars made by the Pullman Palace Car Company. He once showed me an advertising flyer that said that Pullman cars had "All the Comforts of Home." The sleeper cars had beds so that folks didn't have to sleep sitting up on long journeys. Some Pullman cars even had crystal chandeliers hanging over the passengers' heads and soft curtains to wrap around each bed at night. Papa used to say, "Sounds like 'More Comforts Than Home' to me." Then he would wink at Mama. He said that someday he would take her in a Pullman Sleeper Car to see what comforts home should have.

Porters on the trains had the job of greeting the passengers. They also kept the sleeping cars clean, changed the sheets and made the beds, opened and closed the curtains, and even shined passengers' shoes. Oscar said that Pullman Porters were all black men. Most, like himself, had parents or grandparents who had been slaves.

Porters were expected to smile all the time and to keep their white jackets spotless. They had to use their wages to pay for their own uniforms and caps, shoe polish, and shining cloths. Most of the money Porters made came from tips from passengers, so it paid to smile a lot, no matter what passengers asked for.

"As soon as we opened the doors, the passengers would rush into the train and start making requests," Oscar told me. He mimicked the passengers, waving his arms and raising his voice: "Porter, lower my curtain! Boy, when will we get to Portland? George, please check that my bed is made up."

"George?" I asked. "Why did they call you George?"

"Some passengers called us all George because of George Pullman who started the company, just like slaves used to be called by the name of their masters. Smithereens, if that didn't make some Porters crazy! The passengers had all us Porters running up and down the cars until we were all done in." He shook his head at the memory. "But we kept on smiling."

When the train was stopped overnight in a city, Porters had a few hours to sleep. Instead of sleep, Oscar said he'd rather spend his free time and tips on vaudeville shows and operas and moving pictures.

The vaudeville shows had dancers, men who spun plates on their feet, acrobats who walked on their hands, and singers who painted their faces black. I wasn't so sure about what an opera was. The way Oscar talked about it, I figured it was singing that told a story.

I liked it best when he talked about the moving pictures. He described the moving picture *The Great Train Robbery* so many times that I felt I'd seen it myself and could replay it in my dreams. I imagined myself hiding with the masked bandits behind the water tower, waiting for the train to arrive. I wanted so bad to see a moving picture that I could hardly stand it. Oscar told me he would take me to one, if our town ever built a Nickelodeon and my mama let me go.

The main reason Oscar liked being a Pullman Porter was that it was a way to travel all around the country, from the east coast to the west coast to the south and everywhere in between. "I saw the house of Paul Revere in Boston, Massachusetts and alligators in Florida and the peaks of the Rocky Mountains," he said. "I could listen for hours to the clackety clack of the train as it thundered over the mountains. The scenery never grew old and was always pleasing to the eye. I watched and listened to everything and everyone. It was better than any school for learning about all the wonderful things in this world."

There was nothing that Oscar didn't want to know. "I always knew I was different," he said. "My teachers complained that I was too curious. 'Oscar is bright, but he is too inquisitive,' was what they told my mama.

"The other boys nicknamed me 'oddball.' I was an oddball because I read more than they did. I learned more. And I dreamed bigger. I was glad to be an oddball."

I thought about what Miss Farnsworth had told me on my birthday. I knew I could never feel glad to be an oddball. I didn't want people to notice me.

"The funny thing, Tomas, is that being curious isn't always a bad thing. It was a bad thing only at school and at home. Out in the world, being curious is a good thing. Oh, the things I learned on those trains! It was a farmer from Iowa who told me about owning land. One morning I went into his sleeper car, but I couldn't find his shoes to shine. So, being curious, I peeked around his curtain."

Oscar slapped his thigh. "What I saw made me laugh indeed! There he lay, all bundled into his bed in his big fur overcoat and with his shoes on, just as he was when he came into the car the evening before.

"Well, I talked to him a long time. He told me all about farming and the full section of land he owned and how much he paid for it. I knew that I couldn't afford to farm in Iowa where land was expensive, but I could afford to have a homestead in the new and raw part of the country that wasn't yet developed. I decided then and there to 'go west and grow up with the country,' as they say.

"So you see, if I hadn't been curious about where that man's shoes were and found them on his very own feet, I might not have this claim where I now stand."

He said that when he was looking for a relinquished claim, the first locator he found in Bonesteel wouldn't take him to look at claims because of the color of his skin. The next locator told him that the railroad might be extended to the town of Dallas, which was close to Oscar's land. Any town with a railroad stop was sure to grow fast and have a lot of business. Several local towns were fighting to see which one would be the next railroad stop.

The locator introduced Oscar to the banker in Dallas. The banker was a rich man who owned more land than anyone else in Gregory County, and he offered to pay Oscar a lot of money for his relinquishment.

"I told that banker I was here to be a homesteader, not to sell, and that I would make good or die trying," he said. "Don't get me wrong. I can sell anything. Let me tell you!" He laughed. Oscar's laugh was as deep and musical as a church organ.

"When I was just a little older than you are now, my daddy got tired of my poor field work. Back then I wasn't as much interested in working with my hands as much as I wanted to read and learn. With work I wanted to do, I was eager, but other times I was plain lazy. So he told me if I couldn't be of help in the field, I might as well try selling our fruit and vegetables and eggs in town at the open market."

Oscar grinned. "Well, he found out I was what they call a natural salesman. All I needed to do was say something flattering to the ladies, like 'What a lovely hat, Mrs. Jones. Is it new?' Then I'd say, 'Let me show you these fresh double-yolk eggs. I've been holding them just for you.' It worked every time."

Another time he told me about working at the coal mines, earning just thirty cents for every ten thousand pounds of coal he unloaded. "The problem was that I could never unload as much as the other workers. I never earned more than a dollar a day. When the boss told me I could easily unload thirty tons a day if I kept at it, I told him I'd quit before I got to be that good a worker."

One day when we had almost finished building his soddy, Oscar took his wagon to Bonesteel. He came back with several heavy wooden boxes. He'd had the boxes shipped to him on the train from his old home in Chicago. It took both of us to carry them inside.

"Put them in that corner," he said.

"What is in those boxes to make them so heavy?" I asked.

He smiled at me. But for once, he didn't say a word.

Part III:

Strangers in a Strange Land

"The fact that I was a
stranger in a strange land,
inhabited wholly by people not my own race,
did not tend to cheer my gloomy spirits.
I decided it might be all right in July
but never in April."

~ Oscar Micheaux, *The Conquest*

Chapter Seven

South Dakota Gumbo

Now that his soddy was built, Oscar bought mules and a plow. He named the mules Jack and Jenny. We began to break sod on his place. Determined to outdo his neighbors, Oscar worked every day, even in the rain.

The soil in South Dakota was called gumbo, and gumbo gets sticky and balls up when it's wet. It sticks to everything. The muddy gumbo would clump on his plow, so that every few feet the plow would skip and we needed to stop his mules and wipe the mud off the plow blade. Jack and Jenny balked and were ornery. They refused to go where we wanted them to go.

Finally one night I told Joe how Oscar's plow kept getting stuck in the mud. Joe asked what kind of plow we were using. "A square plow," I said.

"Well, no wonder! A square plow won't do at all. He needs a slanted breaker plow to cut through gumbo." Joe shook his head. "That stranger doesn't even know enough to use a breaker plow to break sod."

I wondered why someone would sell Oscar a plow not fit for South Dakota gumbo.

Oscar also had trouble with his horses and mules. The horse he'd bought for traveling was old and had wire cuts on its feet. Oscar didn't know anything about telling a good horse from a bad one.

The work mules he bought were old and untrained. The man who had sold Oscar the mules had coated their hair with dye to make them look younger, but after the first hard rain, the mules' gray hair showed through.

Joe said that folks took advantage of Oscar's being gullible.

Sometimes I saw people watching us from the edge of Oscar's land. They laughed when the plow clumped with buffalo grass. They laughed when his mules were stubborn. He didn't seem to mind that folks pointed at him or tried to cheat him. He just shrugged his shoulders and worked harder.

Oscar's hero was a man named Booker T. Washington, and he quoted him whenever he had the chance. Oscar would say, "Booker T. says that nothing comes to a man except through hard work, and I believe him." Or "Just like Booker T., I let no man drag me down so low as to make me hate him."

"Doesn't it make you angry?" I said one day, after some children had pointed at him and called him names before running away.

"I learned a long time ago that it doesn't pay to get angry," he told me. "It just eats away at your insides and doesn't hurt the person you are angry at. Was it their fault that I got taken in a mule trade? I can tell you that it won't happen to me again. I learned something from my mistake. Someday they will see that Oscar Micheaux is a real homesteader. You just watch. No one will be laughing at me next summer."

"But it's not fair," I argued. I didn't like it when things weren't fair.

He shook his head. "Being fair has nothing to do with it," he replied. "Nothing in life is fair or unfair. All we have is the work we do and the thoughts we think."

That didn't make much sense to me. Certainly being sold the wrong plow wasn't fair. The way people treated him wasn't fair. Joe and Mama sometimes made comments about Oscar that weren't fair, calling him a fool farmer, but I never told him what they said. I even heard Oscar make unfair comments about Joe, saying that Indians didn't work as hard as other folks. But Joe worked harder than almost anyone else I knew. And once in town I heard children making fun of how Mama talked, trying to mimic her accent. That wasn't fair.

Sometimes I felt I didn't understand people very well at all.

In June, the rain finally stopped. The sun shone. Oscar bought a new breaker plow, which allowed him to break land much faster than before. Jack and Jenny were still ornery, but Oscar was learning how to control them.

As much as I enjoyed my time with Oscar, I still spent most of the day at home. Each morning, before the sun began to heat up the air and before I did work for Joe, Winona and Chumani and I planted Mama's garden.

At first, none of us said much as we worked. If I asked a question, the girls would answer by nodding or else with a simple "yes" or "no." They sometimes talked to each other in their language. I tried hard to understand some of the words, but I couldn't. When I heard my name, I knew that they were talking about me, and I didn't like it. When they caught me looking at them, they grew quiet again.

The girls had never been to school, but they could speak English when they wanted to. They just didn't want to most of the time. During these long, quiet mornings I longed for someone to talk to or listen to. Especially when the girls spoke to each other, I felt lonely, worse than if I were alone. I counted the minutes until it was time to walk to Oscar's place.

One morning, Chumani and I were planting turnips. We were careful to spread the tiny seeds evenly over the wide, shallow rows. Winona, walking behind us, used a hoe to cover the seeds with a thin layer of dirt.

Suddenly, Chumani screamed. She was staring at me and screaming so loudly my ears hurt. "Stop it!" I said. Chumani continued to scream. Winona looked at Chumani and then at me. "Stop it!" I said, more loudly. I lifted my hand to slap her. Winona's eyes grew so wide I thought they would explode. She lifted her hoe above her head, and with a yell she brought the hoe down fast and hard in my direction. Before I could defend myself, the blade struck just behind my foot. I screamed, then, too.

When I turned around to look at the hoe stuck in the ground, I saw the head of a rattlesnake next to my boot.

For a moment, we stood still, hardly breathing. The rattlesnake was young, the deadliest kind. Then, all at once, we began to laugh. I laughed so hard that tears ran down my cheeks. Chumani laughed so hard she had to sit down. Winona's laugh echoed behind her like a birdsong as she ran to the soddy. She came back with a knife. With a firm and sure stroke, she cut the rattle off the tail of the snake and tied it in the corner of her shawl.

That night, Winona cut three thin strips of leather from the bottom of one of Chumani's dresses that was too small for her. She braided the leather, carefully weaving it around the rattlesnake rattle and adding some black and gold colored beads. When she gave me the rattle bracelet, she said, "This is to keep snakes away from tall cousin Tomas."

She tied the bracelet on my wrist. She had braided the leather and used the beads in a diamond pattern so that the bracelet looked just like a tiny rattlesnake. I shook my arm. The rattle, now no longer deadly, made a happy sound.

Yes, I thought.

"Cousins," I said.

Chapter Eight

Miss Margaret

In the heat of the summer, a young woman walked to our soddy. She had red hair and green eyes, and her voice was as musical as a songbird. Her name was Margaret O'Reilly. She said to call her Miss Margaret.

"May I come in?" she asked at the doorway, after introducing herself.

Mama invited her to sit at the table. Joe sat with them. I stood just outside the door, chewing on a blade of grass and watching.

"I'm going to start a school, just outside of town," she said. "I'm visiting all of the homesteaders who are within walking distance of the school."

She said to Mama, "Do you have children of school age?"

Mama looked at Joe. "We have two girls, ages nine and six," she said. Winona and Chumani were gathering chokecherries at the creek.

"Why, that is grand!" Miss Margaret said. She did not try to hide her excitement. "The more children, the better. We are starting in the fall, as soon as I get enough books and other supplies. I expect to see them on the first day."

Mama looked at Joe, who was shifting in his chair. She said, "The girls have never been to school."

"Oh, that is no problem," Miss Margaret said. "In fact, some of the other children who will be coming also have not had much schooling."

Joe finally spoke. His voice was slow and measured, like the tick tock of a clock. "It's not that I don't appreciate what you are trying to do, starting this school," he said, "but I know first-hand how schools deal with Indian children."

Miss Margaret stopped smiling for the first time. "Please tell me," she said.

Joe told her all that he had told me during those days when we were building our soddy. Miss

Margaret listened intently, never taking her eyes from him.

"So you see, ma'am," he finished, "while I understand the importance of an education, I will not send my girls to a place where they will learn not only letters and numbers, but also to be ashamed of who they are on the inside."

Miss Margaret looked in her lap and smoothed her dress for several seconds. When she looked back up, she was smiling again, but in a way that was more serious and less cheerful than before.

"Mr. Squirrel Coat, I am sorry for your experience," she said. "I truly am. I know something of the boarding schools for Indian children. I can only promise you that in my classroom, all I care about is helping the children to learn. Who they are on the inside when they come through my door will be the same as who they will be when they go home to you at the end of the day. You do want your girls to know how to read and write, don't you?"

Joe was silent. He seemed to be thinking something over in his head. "We will see," he said.

"That's all I ask, that you think it over," she said. She stood and shook Mama's hand, then Joe's hand. "I would be honored to be their first teacher."

I wondered why Mama hadn't said that I was still of the age to go to school. It was true that I was older than most other pupils, but I had been in schools with boys and girls of twelve and thirteen and even older. Just as I was getting up the courage to ask if I could go to the new school, Mama said, "Tomas, go on down to the creek and see if Winona and Chumani need any help with the chokecherries."

I knew she wanted to talk to Joe about what Miss Margaret had said. I also knew better than to question her.

I met Winona and Chumani as they were coming back from the creek. Their fingers were stained red and purple. They swung pails filled with dark chokecherries. I reached for one to eat, but Winona pushed my hand away.

"These are not good without cooking," she said. "I am going to show ee-nah Sonja how to make them into wojapi." The girls had no problem with calling Mama ee-nah, their word for mother.

"You will like wojapi, cousin Tomas," Chumani added. "It is thick and sweet." She licked her lips.

As much as I usually like to eat and think about food, I couldn't make myself get excited about tasting wojapi. After a while, I asked, "Have you ever wanted to go to school?"

"Oh, no!" Winona said immediately. "Papa told us all about school. Why would I want to go there?"

Chumani didn't answer. "How about you, Chumani?" I asked her. "Would you like to go to school?"

"I don't know," she said. "Not without Winona." She kicked a rock out of her way. "But I would like to know how to read. When I see you reading at night, I wonder about words that go from the pages into your head. They make you look happy."

I had never thought of sharing my newspaper with my new cousins, or that they might like me to read to them.

Chapter Nine

Barn Dance

Late in the summer, the wind began to blow on a Sunday afternoon. It blew all day Monday and all day Tuesday. By Wednesday morning, I couldn't remember what it was like not to hear the wind. By Wednesday night, Mama could no longer keep up with sweeping out the dust that blew under our door and through the holes in our soddy. By Thursday, the wind had blown down our outhouse.

When I woke up on Friday morning, I thought someone had put cotton in my ears. Then I realized the wind had stopped. Everything sounded muffled without the roar of the wind.

I thought I would never again feel clean. My ears and nose were filled with dirt. Dust coated my hair and my clothes. Our beds were coated with dust. Our food tasted like the prairie sod.

Mama said I could go down to the creek to take a bath, even though tomorrow was Saturday. We usually took our baths on Saturday in a tub of heated water, so as to be clean for Sunday.

When I got to the creek, I stripped off my clothes and walked into the water. At first the water was so cold that I walked back out. But I knew that I would soon get used to the cold, so I went back in and walked to the deepest part, which only came up to my ribs. Soon the water felt warmer. I splashed and rubbed myself clean, swishing my hair in the water and wiggling my toes.

When I stepped out, the air made me shiver. I let the breeze dry me as I flapped my clothes in the air to shake out as much dirt as I could. Clean and dry and dressed, I felt like a new person. I walked back to the soddy with a spring in my step.

Joe and I spent the next few days fixing fences and buildings and parts of the garden that had been damaged by the wind. Mama and Winona and Chumani spent almost as long washing all of our clothes and towels and bed linens, rinsing away the dirt and dust.

Joe went to town to buy some food to replace what we had lost to the wind and to get our mail, which was delivered once a week. When he came back, he brought an invitation to a barn dance. He read the invitation to Mama.

The dance was sponsored by the banker and was to be held at his farm south of town. All ages were welcome, and the dance was free.

"Joe, let's go," Mama said. "My family used to go do dances all the time. It would be good for us to get out and enjoy ourselves."

Joe frowned. I could tell he didn't want to go. He wasn't nearly as social as Mama. But he nodded. "For you," was all he said.

All week I thought about the dance.

"Are you going?" I asked Oscar.

"I wouldn't miss it!" he said. He told me that he was having supper in town with the banker before the dance. "I think he still wants to buy my claim."

Finally the day of the dance came. After supper, Mama, Joe, Winona, Chumani, and I put on the clothes we usually reserved for special occasions. We got in the wagon and rode for almost an hour.

The banker's farm was much larger than ours or Oscar's. In addition to a grand, white farm house, he had a bright red wooden barn where the dance was being held. We hitched our horses and wagon to a fence near the barn. Most people were arriving in wagons or on horseback, but a few brand new Ford Model A cars were parked on the side of the barn, as well as the banker's big green luxury Packard car.

Inside the barn, people were gathered near the walls, waiting for the music to begin. Lanterns hung from the ceiling. Sawdust covered the floor. Just like the day in Bonesteel, the voices were a mixture of different languages.

When we heard the fiddlers begin to tune their instruments, a ripple of excitement spread through the barn. Finally the banker thanked everyone for coming and announced that the first dance would begin.

A handful of couples walked to the center of the barn. Everyone else waited, not brave enough to start off the dancing. With a tap of their feet and a loud count of "One! Two! Three!" the fiddlers began to play. Before long, more couples joined in. Soon the barn was alive with music and movement. Everyone seemed to know the language of dance music.

Not quite old enough to dance with the grown-ups and not young enough to join Winona and Chumani with the other children, I found a good spot to watch. Someone brought me a bottle of soda pop, which I had never had before. The sweet liquid fizzled in my mouth.

The sawdust on the floor allowed the dancers to glide as they danced. The men were dressed in their best shirts and the women in fancy dresses. As they kicked their heels and twirled, the dancers formed a swirl of color. Some dancers were very good and never missed a step. These dancers stayed in the center of the barn. Others, on the edges where they wouldn't get in the way, seemed to make up their dance as they went along.

Oscar did not dance with the adults. He entertained the children, who were in the corner of the barn opposite the fiddlers. He sang a song called "Any Rags?" and danced while he sang. "Did you ever hear the story of Ragged, Jagged Jack?" he sang. "Here he comes down the street with a pack on his back." He hunched over and made a face of mock misery. "Any rags, any bones, any bottles today?" he sang. "It's the same old story, in the same old way." The children roared with laughter. He was a good dancer and singer.

Oscar sang and danced with the children all night. The other adults seemed grateful that their children were entertained.

I looked to the dance floor. Miss Margaret was dancing with a young farmer. Mama was trying to show Joe the steps to a folk dance.

Joe was a self-conscious dancer, and he stood with his hands on his hips, stuck in place, unable or unwilling to get his feet to move the right way. I saw that Mama had tears in her eyes and her face was red. I had never seen Mama cry before, not even when Papa had died. A knot formed in my stomach.

"Oh, Joe!" Mama said. She threw her head back and laughed. Joe picked her up by the waist and swung her around.

She was laughing, not crying. I had forgotten what Mama's laughing looked like.

Finally she gave up trying to teach Joe the right steps. Joe brought Mama a cold lemonade, and they moved to an area where couples were talking to each other. They stayed there most of the night, Joe's hand around Mama's waist. Seeing them stand like that made me miss Papa.

Everyone was having such a good time that the banker had to announce at one o'clock in the morning that there would be only one more dance. I had never been up so late at night. After the last stroke of the fiddle, the crowd filed out the barn doors, back to their horses and wagons and cars.

On the way back to our home, Winona and Chumani fell asleep in the back of the wagon, wrapped in blankets. Joe and Mama sat close to each other on the wagon seat, talking softly. I lay on my back next to the girls, rocked by the wagon's back and forth sway, listening to the horses' clip clop on the dirt road.

I studied the stars and looked for constellations and the North Star. I thought about how I could move in the wagon from the banker's farm to our farm—no short distance—but the stars did not move with me. They looked the same, no matter where I was. That was a comforting thought, that some things in the world did not change, or they changed so slowly that we did not notice.

Part IV:

Oscar's Gift

"Few things can help an individual more than
to place responsibility on him,
and to let him know that you trust him."

~ Booker T. Washington

Chapter Ten

Thunderstorm

Early in the fall, before leaves began to change color but after morning air had begun to hang onto the chill of night, Joe announced that Winona and Chumani would go to school.

We were just finishing our noon meal. Mama smiled. Winona and Chumani looked at each other but said nothing.

"Can I go to the new school, too?"

I hadn't planned to ask. The words just came out.

Mama stopped smiling. She got up from the table and began to clear the plates. Joe sighed, then said, "I can't spare you, Tomas. We still have more than half of the claim to break. You are a farmer now, son, not a school child."

I looked at Mama. I never had begged for anything before, but I let my eyes beg now. Please, I willed my eyes to say to her across the room. Please.

"Your father is right. We need you on the farm, Tomas."

Before I could stop myself, I yelled, "He's not my father!" I turned to Joe. "And I'm not your son! Never call me that again!"

"Tomas!" Mama's voice came down as hard as an axe. The look on her face was worse than if I'd slapped her. I turned on my heels and left the soddy, slamming the door behind me.

The day was hot and ripe for a thunderstorm, just as I felt inside, as if any moment the sky would burst open and drench the world with its ripeness. For now, though, there was no rain. The air was heavy and still. A thick line of dark clouds sat low in the western horizon, waiting, gathering strength.

It was too early in the day for me to help Oscar, but it was the only place I could go. As I walked, I thought about what I had said. If Papa were alive, he would be very angry with me. But if Papa were alive, he would let me go to school. I knew he would. I raised my face to the sky and yelled until my throat was sore. I hit my fists against my legs. Finally I slowed my pace, but my thoughts raced faster than ever. I didn't know what to do or where to go. I didn't know what to say when I saw Mama again. Most of all, I didn't how to stop myself from feeling so angry.

I would ask Oscar what to do. He would know.

Oscar was not in his soddy when I arrived at his place. He wasn't working in his garden. He wasn't finishing building the milking stalls in his barn. He wasn't in his necessary house.

I walked to the back of the barn where I saw Jenny the mule walking toward me. Her harness reins trailed on the ground. She was dragging the breaking plow behind her.

"What is the matter, Jenny? Where is Oscar?" I said more to myself than to the mule. I unhitched the plow, removed Jenny's harness, and put her in a stall in the barn.

I followed the trail made by the plow. The mule had dragged the plow through Oscar's garden, tearing up newly planted pumpkin hills. She had pulled the plow across the new alfalfa crop, chewing up the tender young shoots. The winding trail of broken dirt and plants finally led me to Oscar.

He lay flat on his back on the ground, his legs and arms splayed outward. Blood ran in a stream down his face.

"Oscar!" I cried.

I tried to lift him, but he was too heavy.

"Wake up. Please wake up." I grabbed his leg and shook it, but he didn't open his eyes. I held his head off the ground and wrapped my kerchief around a large gash on his forehead. As gently as I could, I lowered his head back to the dirt. I leaned close to his ear. "I'll be back real soon," I said. "Wait here."

I ran as fast as I could back to our place. I barged through our door, nearly falling over. Mama and the girls were kneading bread dough. They stopped when they saw me, their hands stuck in the soft white mounds.

"Goodness, Tomas! What is the matter with you today?" Mama asked.

"It's Osc—Mr. Micheaux!" I said, trying to catch my breath. "He is hurt and bleeding! I think his mule kicked him."

As fast as a garter snake Mama whipped off her apron and grabbed a handful of clean sack cloths from the cupboard.

"Finish the bread," she told Chumani.

"Go to the barn and gather as many spider webs as you can find," she told Winona. "Bring them to Mr. Micheaux's soddy when you have a good handful."

She looked to where I was still standing in the doorway. "Come with me," she said.

We filled a jar with water from the rain barrel. On our way to Oscar's place we pulled some milkweed plants. I didn't know that Mama could walk so fast. I had to jog to keep up with her.

Oscar was still lying on the ground when we reached him. Mama knelt beside him. She carefully unwrapped my kerchief from his head. The blood was beginning to cake around his wound and was no longer running down his face. He moaned and opened his eyes.

"Be still," Mama ordered.

She didn't have to tell him. Oscar looked straight up. His eyes were big and round.

She dipped the corner of a cloth in the water and used it to wipe away the blood. She wrapped a clean cloth around his head and poured a little water on his lips.

Finally he turned his eyes to me, then to Mama. He reached for the water jar.

"Slowly, Mr. Micheaux," Mama said.

When he had drunk some water, Mama asked him if he could stand. He nodded. Mama and I stood on each side of him and helped him to his feet. He leaned heavily on me, trying to put less of his weight on Mama's side.

We made our way step by step across the field, stopping often for Oscar to rest or drink some water. The short trip seemed to take hours. Blood began to ooze through the cloth and drip down his cheek again.

Winona was waiting outside the door when we finally reached the soddy.

We all went inside. Mama and I lowered Oscar to his bed. When his head met his pillow, he closed his eyes and moaned again. She lifted the cloth from his wound. Once again she cleaned up the blood.

Mama snapped a milkweed stem in half. She held a broken end right above Oscar's forehead and let the milky white sap drip on his wound.

"Did you bring the spider webs?" she asked Winona.

Winona reached in the pocket of her skirt and pulled out a kerchief. Wrapped inside was a mass of spider webs.

Mama used her fingers to form some of the spider webs into a soft bandage. She placed this web bandage on the milkweed sap. She used another clean cloth to wrap around Oscar's forehead again.

Through all of this, Oscar slept.

"Tomas, you stay here with him tonight. When he wakes up, give him some water and some bread if he wants it. Not too much. Don't let him stand or walk until tomorrow."

I nodded.

Outside the thunder cracked and we all jumped, all except Oscar. He was so still I was afraid he was no longer alive.

Mama turned to Winona. "We must go home now." Winona gave me a look that said she wished she could stay with me. I managed a small smile.

Alone, I noticed the unusual darkness for late afternoon. I stepped outside. Black clouds moved and swirled above me, a boiling muddy sky streaked with lightning. A large raindrop splashed on my nose.

I ran to the barn to make sure that Jack, Jenny, and Oscar's horse were inside and had enough hay and water. By the time I ran back to the soddy, the sky had cracked open and rain was pouring so hard it hurt when it hit my skin. Thunder echoed everywhere. I shut the door behind me.

I sat next to Oscar's bed and listened to the storm. Oscar slept through all the thunder and rain, but I didn't sleep a wink that night. Sometime before the sun came up, the rain stopped and the wind died down.

Oscar finally opened his eyes when morning light streamed through the windows.

He touched the cloth on his forehead. "What happened?" he asked, his voice so soft and hoarse I could barely hear him.

"I'm not sure," I said, "but I think that Jenny kicked you in the head."

"Darned mule!" he croaked. "She was always watching me out of her left eye." He breathed heavily. "She had the last laugh after all."

I changed Oscar's bandage and helped him to drink some water. Just as I was cutting a slice of bread for him to eat, there was a knock at the door.

"That's probably Mama," I said.

But it wasn't Mama. It was one of Oscar's neighbors, a short, fat woman with several children hiding behind her large skirt. I recognized her from the barn dance. She stood in the doorway and handed me a jar of soup.

"Sonja told us what happened," she said. "I thought you might like something warm to eat while you recover." Her skirt rustled as her children strained to look around her to get a peek at Oscar.

Oscar managed a smile and nodded in gratitude. I put the soup on the table. The neighbor left, but soon there was another knock on the door and another neighbor, this time bringing some fresh bread. Then another with wild plum jelly.

All morning folks stopped by to bring Oscar food or to see if he needed anything. They seemed both concerned to see if he was alright and curious as to how this strange homesteader lived.

Mama and Joe visited for a while, too. Joe told Oscar that he would help him to trade his mules for work horses that were trained to pull farm machinery.

In the afternoon, Oscar slept. By evening he was feeling well enough to change his own bandage and walk to his necessary house.

"You go on home now, Tomas. Tell your mama I don't need any more nursing," he said.

I was so tired that I didn't try to change his mind. I nearly fell asleep as I walked home in the dark. When I opened the door to our soddy, Mama greeted me with a hug. I didn't mind, even though I was too old for hugs.

Neither Mama nor Joe ever said a word to me about my angry words. The storm had blown my anger far away and left in its wake a new calm.

Chapter Eleven

First Day of School

On their first day of school, Winona and Chumani wore new deerskin dresses decorated simply with ribbons and fringe. The cream-colored deerskin was as soft as a kitten. Mama scrubbed their faces, brushed and braided their hair, and tied matching ribbons on the ends of their braids. She gave them each a dinner pail.

"Go on with Tomas, now. He will meet you at the end of the day and walk you home."

Mama looked at me in a way that made me feel proud. She trusted me to look after my cousins, to keep them safe.

We walked in silence in the crisp morning air. The cottonwoods in the distance had begun to turn from green to golden yellow. The prairie grasses were fading to brown. The earth felt hard beneath my feet, as if preparing itself for colder months to come. Even the blue of the sky was muted, a faded version of the deeper hue of mid-summer.

The school was past Oscar's land. He saw us from where he was sharpening the blades of his plow. He waved at us. I waved back. Except for a scar on his forehead, he was fully recovered from being kicked in the head by his mule. He now had reliable work horses for farming instead of old, or-nery mules.

We continued walking. Winona looked straight ahead, her face as still as stone. Chumani glanced nervously between me and Winona. When we rounded a hill and saw the school house, both girls stopped. Winona turned to me.

"Cousin Tomas, you can be our teacher. We don't need a school or Miss Margaret." Her eyes were wet with tears, but she did not allow them to fall down her cheek. Chumani looked at the ground.

I did not know what to do. I wanted to walk into the school and tell Miss Margaret that they were scared, that they were good girls and to be patient because they had never sat in a desk or learned to read. I wanted to tell the other pupils not to stare at them and never to make fun of them. I wanted to grab their hands and run with them back to our home where they could remain invisible.

Then I remembered the look Mama had given me and my responsibility.

I took a deep breath and knelt down beside them. "I know you are scared," I said. "I was scared every time I went to a new school, too. And I went to a lot of schools."

"How many?" Winona asked.

"More than I even remember," I said. "I learned a lot in those schools, and I'm glad I went to every one of them. But the most important thing I learned was that the only way not to feel scared is to walk right through it. Walk through the scared feeling until you come through the other side."

Chumani finally looked up at me. Her eyes were dry. I shook my bracelet. "You don't have to worry about me today. I'm safe from rattlesnakes until I come to meet my brave cousins to walk me home."

Chumani looked at Winona and took her hand. Together they walked away from me into a new world.

I watched them approach the door of the school house. They held their heads high. The ribbons in their braids bounced against the backs of their dresses.

Miss Margaret met them at the door. She bent down and smiled, and although I couldn't hear what she was saying, I knew she was asking their names. She looked up and saw me in the distance. She waved. It was okay for me to walk back home.

What I did not tell Winona and Chumani was that I would have done almost anything to have taken their place.

On my way home, I stopped at Oscar's claim. He was inside his soddy with the door open to let in light. He sat at his table, writing in a notebook. I tapped on the open door. He looked up.

"Tomas!" he said with a grin. Oscar always was happy to see me.

"Good morning," I said. I stared at his notebook. I wanted to ask what he was writing, but Mama said it wasn't polite to ask people questions.

Oscar seemed to know what I was thinking. "I'll bet you wonder what I'm writing and why I'm not farming."

I felt my cheeks turn red. I nodded.

"What if I told you I am farming?" he said. "And that while I am in the field, I am also writing?"

This sounded like one of the riddles in *The Youth's Companion*. I wasn't sure how to answer, so I asked, "Are you planning your crops for next spring?"

"No, something even better."

He waited, so as to see me look puzzled. Then he said, "I'm planting words."

He motioned for me to sit next to him. "This grand prairie"—he swept his hand toward the door—"is like a blank piece of paper. The way I see it, we come here to write our story on the land, acre by acre. Every homesteader's claim tells a different tale."

"What is your tale?" I asked.

Oscar grinned. "I'm still writing it," he said.

I told Oscar about how I had once thought I would be a newspaper man. I told him about *The*

Youth's Companion and how much I missed school. I had never talked about these things before, not even to Mama, and the words rushed out like a river overflowing its banks. I told him about how my father had wanted me to work with my head instead of my hands. I told him that Papa would be disappointed in me now.

"Ah, Tomas, there is your problem," he said. "You see working with your head and your hands as being two different things. But, for a writer, they are one and the same. After all, we write with our hands, don't we? In the words of Booker T., 'there is as much dignity in tilling a field as in writing a poem.'

"Being a writer is no different from being a homesteader. Both writers and homesteaders start with blank paper and blank land. We use tools of pens and plows. We start at the beginning and work our way to the other side, solving problems and meeting new characters along the way. No experience is wasted for a writer or a farmer. No moment is lost."

"Will you let me read what you are writing?" I asked.

"Not now, but, yes, someday," he said. "When my tale is finished."

I left Oscar to continue his tale. As I walked to meet Joe for the morning's work, I decided that if Oscar could write his own future, I could, too. I just needed to find a way.

Chapter Twelve

More Birthday Surprises

I was awake before I opened my eyes. The cool morning air felt good on my face. I smelled cobs burning in the monkey stove and heard Winona and Chumani whispering on the other side of the soddy. I wanted to enjoy my own thoughts for a few more minutes, so I lay as still as I could and pretended to be asleep.

Last year on this day I had no idea that I would wake up on my thirteenth birthday in a home that I had helped to build. That day, which seemed so very long ago, I had walked to school, not knowing that it would be my last day in a classroom. I also could not have known that soon I would be needed to help two girls to go to their own first day of school.

Back then I felt that life was not my own, that I was like a tumbleweed blown across the prairie, occasionally getting stuck in a fence or caught in a tree, but mostly bouncing from place to place without a clear direction. Even what most people would consider good luck—winning the land lottery—I had seen as just another way that life was unfair.

While I was ashamed to admit it, instead of feeling happy for Mama when she married Joe, I felt sorry for myself for not having a father. I couldn't even see that Winona and Chumani really had suffered the same loss I had. It didn't matter whether they had known their mother. They still had a hole in their lives, and they needed someone to fill it. In that way, they were indeed my sisters.

Now I was a farmer, just like Mama had said I would be. A real farmer.

And on this morning as I looked forward to the coming day, Miss Farnsworth's words came back to me: "You have been given a gift with words, Tomas. A boy like you has a different kind of future from a lot of others. You are lucky. You have to know what you want and be willing to work to get it."

My thoughts were interrupted by an urgent voice.

"Cousin Tomas, wake up!" Chumani could no longer wait for me. She nudged my shoulder until I opened one eye.

"Get out of bed! We have presents for you." Her face was aglow with expectation. Since starting school, she had become even more bubbly, so unlike her sister and father. I wondered if she was like her mother.

I made a big show of yawning and rubbing my eyes. "Leave an old man to his sleep," I teased. Chumani's laughter rang throughout the soddy like sleigh bells.

I pulled on my trousers over my long johns and a work shirt over my night shirt. As I reached for my boots, Winona used her foot to push them beyond my reach. She stood in front of me, holding her hands behind her. She was as calm as Chumani was exuberant.

"This morning you will wear something softer than hard boots that are too big for you," she said.

From behind her back she brought a pair of moccasins. She placed them at my feet.

They were decorated with porcupine quills dyed blue and green. I recognized the soft brown leather from the dress that was too small for Chumani. Winona had designed the pattern of quills on the front of the moccasins to match the diamond pattern of my bracelet. The laces were cut from the same leather as the dress. Thin fringe strung with tiny beads hung from the top of each moccasin.

I put them on my feet. They fit perfectly. They felt like stepping into soft sand. Chumani clapped her hands with glee. She said, "Winona measured your foot while you were sleeping. Your feet always stick out of your blanket." She giggled.

It was true. My old wool blanket, meant for a child, was now too short for me, and I often woke up with cold feet and toes if I forgot to wear stockings to bed.

Before I could say thank you, Chumani reached under her mattress and brought out a large sack. Too impatient to give it to me, she pulled out a folded blanket.

"This used to belong to our ee-nah," she said. "Ah-tay said you need it now and can have it, but only if you promise to stop growing." She handed me the blanket.

I unfolded the blanket, which was more than long enough to cover my feet and toes. The blanket, which I thought at first was made of cloth, was instead a soft, tanned buffalo hide. In the center was a large circle, painted in black and white. Surrounding the circle were carefully painted scenes of young Indian braves racing bareback across on the prairie on horses, spears at their sides. They rode round and round the circle forever, chasing an unseen buffalo herd.

I could not speak.

"Tomas," Mama said, "come here, please."

I knew she would tell me to be polite, and would chide me for not thanking Winona and Chumani for such beautiful, generous gifts. But my tongue was stuck. I was afraid that if I tried to say anything, I would cry, and I could not cry in front of the girls.

I refolded the blanket and put it on my mattress, then sat beside Mama at the table. She held out her hand.

She did not scold me. She was holding the watch Papa had always carried in his pocket, the one that he always put on his dresser before he went to bed. It was the watch the man with the telegram had brought to her the day when he died.

"Tomas, this watch was not only your father's, but his father's and his father's before that. Now it is yours. It is a Swedish watch, the best watch there is. Someday you can give it to your own son, and he can give it to his son."

While I had seen Papa look at his watch and take it in and out of his pocket hundreds of times, I had never seen it up close. The face was white and the hands were gold. The numbers were black and elegant. The words "Lundstedt Stockholm" were written in script on the bottom.

I put the watch in my pocket and stood up. "Thank you," I finally managed to say.

In that moment, I felt that nothing could make this birthday better.

After a breakfast of flapjacks and wojapi, I milked Maggie. When I returned to the soddy, I saw Chumani and Mama sitting at the table, a book opened in front of them. Chumani held Mama's finger under the words as she read them: "A cat. A rat. A cat and a rat. A rat and a cat." They were reading together. I hadn't noticed that while I was working with Oscar every evening, the girls must be helping Mama to learn alongside them.

Joe came in from his morning chores. "I will take the girls to school this morning," he said to me. "You go to help Oscar early today."

Not until I was halfway to Oscar's place did I think that he would be surprised to see me so early in the day. He might be in town for the morning. Or he might already be in the field.

But he was sitting outside his soddy, as if he expected me.

"Tomas, you are looking quite tall this morning," he said, his eyes twinkling.

I grinned.

"Come inside," he said.

Oscar had dragged the boxes I had helped him to unload from his wagon last spring to the middle of his floor. A crowbar lay beside them.

"Open them," he said.

I looked at him to be sure he was serious, then I knelt beside the closest box and pried off the lid.

The lid came off with a loud creak and a small cloud of dust and packing straw. Inside were books. More books than I'd ever seen in one place. More books than I'd seen even in a school. No wonder the boxes were so heavy.

"Go on!" Oscar said. "I don't have all day." He laughed.

I took out the books, one by one, looking through the pages before placing the book on the floor and taking out another. Some were books about the wild west, with drawings of cowboys and gun fights on the cover. Some were books about businesses and oil companies, or the lives of famous people. Some books didn't have pictures. Some did. Some didn't have titles on the cover, but the titles were printed on the inside pages. I looked at every book, inside and out, as I emptied the box.

I opened a second box. It contained Farmer's Bulletins about planting crops and raising farm animals and harvesting corn and wheat. I opened a third and a fourth box. There was *Up from Slavery* by Booker T. Washington, and *The Souls of Black Folk* by a man named W. E. B. DuBois.

I took out book after book after book until the sod floor of his house was covered with books. The only other time I had felt such utter contentment was when Miss Farnsworth had given me *The Youth's Companion*. Even though these were Oscar's books, not mine, just being around them made me feel less lonely, less different. The books felt like friends. By the look on Oscar's face, I knew he felt the same way.

Oscar said, "Tomas, I'd like to give you a raise, to start paying you more for your work. I know you give your wages to your mama. And it is right that you do. I'd give my wages to my mama, too, if I were in your place. But I want to pay you something that is only yours."

He looked at me for a sign that I understood. I nodded.

"I will give you three dollars a week instead of two," he said, "and, if you want, I will also let you read any of these books you fancy and we can talk about them while we work together. You can take them home, as long as you return them when you are finished. Does that sound fair to you?"

This time I was not at a loss for words.

"Oh, yes!" I said.

Oscar shook my hand.

"It's a deal, then," he said.

We took apart the boxes and used the boards to build bookcases. We lined the walls of the soddy with the bookcases and arranged the books by author on the shelves. Every part of the walls not covered by other furniture was now covered with books.

"What work do you have for me today?" I asked when we were finished.

Oscar frowned. "Some difficult work, just for today," he said. His eyes sparkled in the way they did when he said one thing and meant another. "Choose one of these books and don't come back until tomorrow afternoon."

He waited patiently while I made my choice. I read the first pages of several books until I finally found one that described a man looking out the window of a Pullman railroad car. "Through the window-glass of our Pullman the thud of their mischievous hoofs reached us, and the strong, humorous curses of the cow-boys," I read. "Then for the first time I noticed a man who sat on the high gate of the corral, looking on. For he now climbed down with the undulations of a tiger, smooth and easy, as if his muscles flowed beneath his skin."

Oscar nodded his approval. I tucked *The Virginian* under my arm. Then, as some men do, Oscar and I said goodbye without needing to say a word.

Luck is a funny thing. I used to think I was unlucky because Papa had died and my world had changed without my permission. But now, because of those changes, I had three fathers: my beloved Papa, whose watch I would always feel in my pocket, keeping me on time and connected to my past. Joe, who was able to make Mama laugh again, even if he didn't smile or laugh himself. And my friend Oscar, whose gift of words matched my own.

About halfway home, I climbed to the top of a flat, grassy plateau. From there I could see the young town of Dallas to the south where the railroad might be built. I saw our claim on one side of me and Oscar's claim on the other. I saw the brown buffalo grass and the patchwork of plowed fields and the gentle sloping hills scattered like huge walnut shells across the prairie, each one a treasure for the homesteaders who live here. I saw the rows of cottonwood trees standing proud against the creek banks, their branches reaching one hundred feet into the sky. I heard their heart-shaped golden leaves flutter in the wind and saw them glisten like glass trinkets in the setting sun. They may not have been gold coins, but they were just as precious.

I knew I was standing on the edge of something strange and new and beautiful.

Epilogue:

What Happened Afterward

For two years after my thirteenth birthday I used Oscar's books to teach myself to be a better writer. Oscar showed me how to copy paragraphs that I liked and study them until their rhythms were a part of my thoughts. I wrote new endings to my favorite stories, and I wrote stories I had made up in my head. I even wrote a story about the boys who made arrowheads and hunted buffalo. Just like breaking sod, I broke and planted new words every day. And just like breaking sod, it took time to see the fruits of my labor.

Joe did raise hogs and buy chickens. Eventually he earned enough money to build a two-story wooden house just like the one I used to imagine before Papa died. He hired a farm worker to help him with the animals and crops. He still has not cut his hair, and he continues to make Mama laugh.

The summer when I was fifteen, I began to work as an apprentice at the newspaper. Within two years I was indeed a real and true newspaper man. Since then I have traveled all across the country. I visited the places in Chicago that Oscar told me about. I saw moving pictures, including *The Great Train Robbery*. I interviewed important people and wrote newspaper stories about them. I also got married and have two children. We named them Sonya and Oscar.

Winona and Chumani stayed in school and went to high school. Winona moved to the western part of South Dakota, where she is married and has two beautiful daughters. Chumani became a school teacher, and she teaches at the same school that she and Winona first attended. She is known far and wide for her good nature and laughter.

And what about Oscar? He worked as a homesteader for six more years, buying even more claims and breaking more acres than other, more experienced farmers. Before lack of rain and drought eventually forced him to quit farming and sell his land, he had earned the respect and friendship of the other homesteaders.

After he left South Dakota, I didn't see or hear from him for a while. Then, recently, I received a parcel in the mail. I unwrapped the brown paper, and inside was a book titled *The Conquest: The Story of a Negro Pioneer*. It was dedicated to "the Honorable Booker T. Washington." Beneath the dedication, Oscar had hand written, "To Tomas, who shares my love of stories and books. Please accept this gift from me."

About Oscar Micheaux

Tomas, his father, Sonya, Joe, Winona, Chumani, Miss Farnsworth, Mrs. Sully and Miss Margaret are fictional characters. Oscar Micheaux, however, was a real person. He was born in 1883 in Metropolis, Illinois. He really did work as a Pullman Porter, go to Bonesteel for the land lottery in 1904 and buy a relinquished claim when his lottery number wasn't chosen.

He continued to homestead for several years in South Dakota until the drought of 1911 made farming too difficult. In 1913 he published *The Conquest: The Story of a Negro Pioneer*, a novel based on his years on the prairie. Oscar went on to publish several more novels. He also taught himself the craft of filmmaking and established the Micheaux Book and Film Company. He is considered to be the first African American feature-length film producer. All told, he wrote seven novels and produced forty-four films, twenty-two silent films and twenty-two talkies.

He died in 1951 in North Carolina.

Activities & Discussion Questions

1. Were you surprised to learn that Tomas's mother could not read or write? Why or why not?

2. Visit The Youth's Companion Project to see the full August 18, 1904 issue. Click on "The Library" for a list of all available online issues:
   http://youthscompanion.com/

3. Are buffalo the same as bison? Were what Tomas called buffalo really buffalo? How can you find the answer?

4. View a photo collection of sod buildings, including homes, barns, and churches:
   http://memory.loc.gov/ammem/award97/ndfahtml/hult_sod.html

5. Can you think of an example of when you have felt like an oddball? What makes someone an "odd-ball"?

6. Watch *The Great Train Robbery*:
   http://www.archive.org/details/the-great-trainrobbery

7. Learn to make wojapi!
   http://www.aihd.ku.edu/recipes/wojapi.html

8. Learn some Lakota Sioux words:
   http://www.lakhota.org/downloads/pdf/Lakota%20Alphabet.pdf

9. How would you describe Tomas's personality? Chumani's? Winona's?

10. Have you ever wanted to do something that didn't seem possible? Do you have a gift for doing something special?

Visit http://lisarivero.com for more learning and discussion resources, a teaching guide, and links to historical photographs that are included in the ebook version of *Oscar's Gift*.

About the Author

Lisa Rivero grew up on a farm on the same South Dakota Rosebud Indian Reservation where Oscar Micheaux homesteaded. There she attended a two-room country school and was one of three students in her class. Like Tomas, she knew she wanted to be a writer from a young age. As an adult, Lisa is a college writing teacher at Milwaukee School of Engineering and an award-winning author of four previous books on education and parenting.

http://lisarivero.com